KT-437-131

In everyone there sleeps
a sense of life lived according to love.
Philip Larkin

for David Lloyd
J. D.

for all at Craigmillar
Books for Babies
P. B.

First published 2009 by Walker Books Ltd, 87 Vauxhall Walk, London SE11 5HJ

10 9 8 7 6 5 4 3 2 1

Text © 2009 Joyce Dunbar Illustrations © 2009 Patrick Benson

The right of Joyce Dunbar and Patrick Benson to be identified as author and illustrator
respectively of this work has been asserted by them in accordance with the Copyright,
Designs and Patents Act 1988.

This book has been typeset in Gill Sans Schoolbook.

Printed in China

All rights reserved. No part of this book may be reproduced, transmitted or stored
in an information retrieval system in any form or by any means, graphic,
electronic or mechanical, including photocopying, taping and recording,
without prior written permission from the publisher.

British Library Cataloguing in Publication Data:
a catalogue record for this book is available
from the British Library.

ISBN 978-1-84428-032-2

www.walker.co.uk

MORAY COUNCIL LIBRARIES & INFO.SERVICES	
20 26 94 64	
Askews	
JA	

oddly

joyce
dunbar

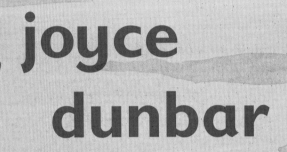

illustrated by

patrick
benson

WALKER BOOKS
AND SUBSIDIARIES
LONDON · BOSTON · SYDNEY · AUCKLAND

Round and round in circles went the Lostlet.
"Where am I? Where am I? Where am I?" he sighed.
He twirled a big golden leaf in his hand.
"What I hope… What I hope… What I hope…"
But he didn't know what he was hoping for
so he fell silent.

In and out of shadows skipped the Strangelet.
"What am I? What am I? What am I?" he murmured.
He held a smooth white pebble in his hand.
"What I dream… What I dream… What I dream…"
But he didn't know what he was dreaming of
so he went quiet.

Dancing in the wavelets went the Oddlet.
"Who am I? Who am I? Who am I?" he whispered.
He listened to the pink shell at his ear.
"What I wish… What I wish… What I wish…"
But he didn't know what he was wishing for
so he stopped still.

Running down the road came the little boy. "Where am I? What am I? Who am I?" he cried.

The Lostlet stopped in his tracks.

The Strangelet blinked with surprise.

The Oddlet
flipped right over.

What was this? Who was this?

How did he come to be here?

Stranger, odder, more lost than they.

A boy. Never in their lost,
strange, odd little worlds
had they ever seen a boy.

The little boy sat down and cried.

The Lostlet ran up to him.

"Hush!" he murmured.

The Strangelet sat beside him.

"Shush!" he whispered.

The Oddlet peered up at the boy.

"What's that noise you are making?" he asked.

"I'm lost," said the boy.

"I ran away so far

that I can't find my way home."

"Home?" said the Lostlet. "What means home?"
"Home is where I live," said the boy.

"Live?" said the Strangelet. "What means live?"
"I want my Mum," sniffed the boy.

"Mum?" said the Oddlet. "What means Mum?"
The boy cried louder than ever.
"I want some love," he sobbed.

"Love? What means love?" said the Strangelet.

"Can you hold it?" asked the Strangelet.
"Can you twirl it?" asked the Lostlet.
"Can you hear it?" asked the Oddlet.

The boy blinked back his tears.
"Love is what makes you better," said the boy.

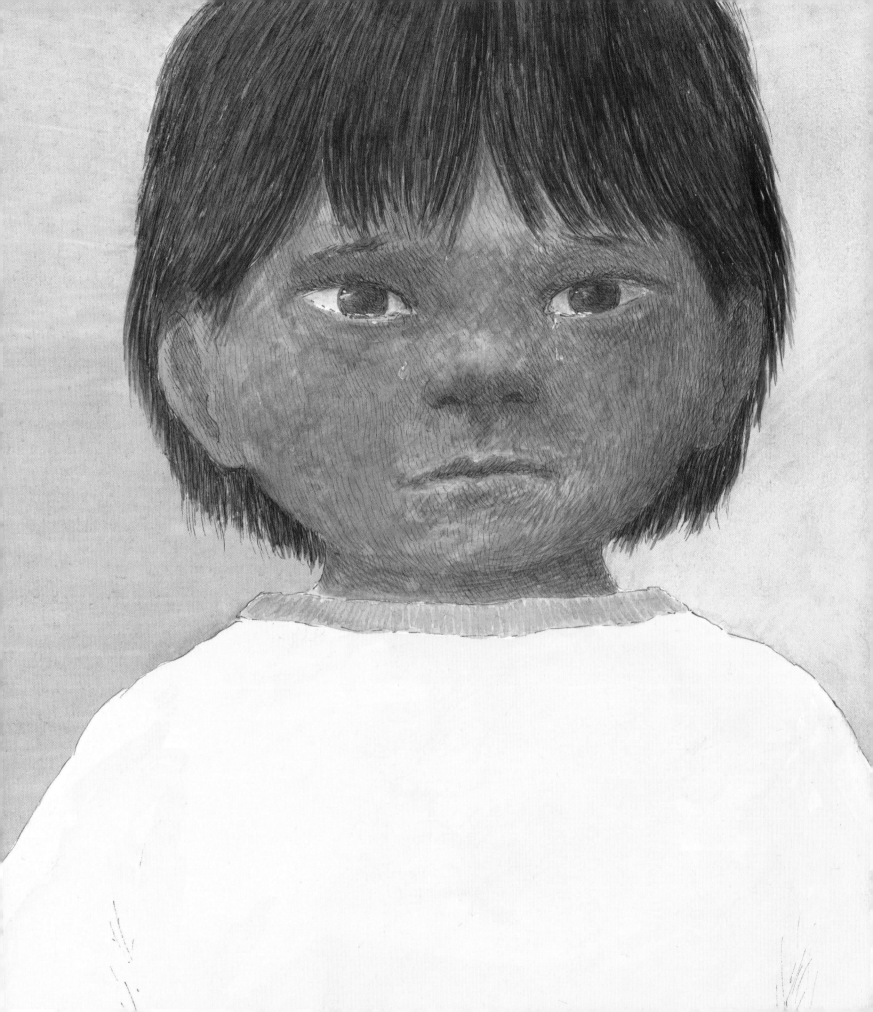

"I don't know about love," said the Lostlet,
"but you can have my golden leaf to twirl.
It's my twirliest leaf."
"And you can have my white pebble to hold,"
said the Strangelet. "It's my favourite pebble."
"And you can put my pink shell to your ear,"
said the Oddlet. "It's my best shell."

The little boy stopped crying.
He twirled the golden leaf.
He held the white pebble.
He put the pink shell to his ear.

To the Oddlet he gave a hug.

The Oddlet went very pink.

"So that's what I've been wishing for," he said.

"I'm a Huglet!"

To the Strangelet he gave a cuddle.

The Strangelet felt a deep warm glow.

"So that's what I've been dreaming of," he chuckled.

"I'm a Snuglet!"

He took the Lostlet by the hand.

The Lostlet gave a shy smile.

"So that's what I've been hoping for," he said.

"I'm a Foundlet!"

Dancing in a ring they sang a little song.

"A Huglet am I, odd though I be,
A Snuglet so strange, you never did see,
Lostlets no more, all found are we.
How we hope...
    How we wish...
        How we dream ..."
"to be HOME," finished the boy,
with a twirl of the
golden leaf.

Strangely...
    Suddenly...
        Oddly ...

they **were** home ...

just in time for supper.